Hundred-Acre Adventures
Nap Time

Ladybird

It was a lovely, sunny summer afternoon. All of the friends of the Hundred-Acre Wood were gathered around Tigger, who was explaining how a tigger's springy tail makes them the best bouncers.

Suddenly, Kanga called out to her son. 'Roo! I'm waiting for you, sweetheart!'

Roo pretended he didn't hear.

'Well, Roo,' said Rabbit, 'something tells me it is time for your nap.'

'Are you sure it's nap time?' grumbled a frowning Roo.

'Same time as yesterday, darling,' replied Kanga.

'But I don't feel like taking a nap right now. Couldn't I take one later? I'll sleep extra to catch up, like this.' Roo shut his eyes tightly and made a funny face.

Owl cleared his throat. 'I'm afraid that won't do any good. As my wise old grandmother used to say, if you don't have a proper nap you'll run out of play before the end of the day.'

But Roo ignored Owl and burst out laughing. Tigger had bundled him up and sent him flying like a ball up into the air and back down again.

Kanga held out her arms to catch her little one.

'Time to go now, Roo.'

'Just a minute,' Roo replied. 'I'm playing a bouncing game with Tigger.'

'Remember what Owl said about running out of play!' said Rabbit.

'But I've got heaps left!' Roo grumbled, 'I don't need to nap for more.'

'Anyway, I still don't understand why I should go now,' argued Roo. 'I'm just not tired.'

'We all need lots of rest when we're small,' said Piglet.

Roo pointed up to the sky. 'But nobody else sleeps during the day! The sun doesn't sleep, the sky doesn't sleep, the flowers and the bees don't… '

'Owls sleep during the daytime, Roo,' reasoned Owl.

'Well, at least you get to stay up **all** night to make up for it,' Roo complained.

'You know,' said Pooh, 'I very much like taking afternoon naps, especially after eating a pot of honey.'

'Hey!' added Tigger. 'Just think how much more bouncy you'll feel after a nap!'

With that Tigger threw his paws in the air and twisted his tail in an enormous bounce, landing right on top of poor Eeyore's house.

'Well, I could do with a little nap,' grumbled Eeyore. 'Except now I can't because I don't have a house to nap in.'

Roo looked at Eeyore in surprise. 'Why don't all of you take a nap if you like it so much? I don't want to be the only one asleep while everyone else gets to play.'

'Play?' cried Rabbit. 'We've got work to do!'

'We do?' asked Tigger, surprised.

'Yes we do!' Rabbit laughed. 'Thanks to your silly bouncing we've got to rebuild poor Eeyore's house.'

'Thanks for noticing that,' said Eeyore, gloomily.

'So I won't be missing out?' asked Roo, with a little yawn.

'Not a single bounce!' grinned Tigger, as he jumped through the window, right onto Roo's bed.

Rabbit started collecting lots of sticks straight away.

'Oh bother,' said Pooh as he struggled with two especially awkward ones. 'This is going to be tricky.'

'There's so much to do I don't know where to start!' Piglet cried, following behind.

'Have a good nap!' all of Roo's friends exclaimed, waving goodbye as they set to work.

Once Tigger had sprung back out of the window, Kanga put Roo into bed. 'Sweet dreams, darling!' she whispered.

'We'll play lots of games when I wake up, won't we, Mama?' said Roo, as his head sank into the soft pillow.

'Oh yes,' nodded Kanga as she closed the door, 'Lots and lots of games.'

As soon as he heard the door shut, Roo sat up.

'I'm still not ready to fall asleep,' he said.

Roo climbed out of bed and picked up his toys.

'It's time for you all to take a nap while I do some work!' he declared, sitting on the bed to watch them. Soon he realised the toys weren't behaving. Each time he wriggled, they wriggled too.

'Mummy lies down next to me to help me sleep,' he remembered. 'I'll lie down next to you so that you can take your nap.'

Soon little Roo was fast asleep too, dreaming of sticks, houses and bouncing games…

It was late in the afternoon when Roo woke from his nap. He bounced out of bed and into the kitchen. Kanga had prepared a delicious snack for him – a glass of juice, some bread with mustard and a hot bowl of soup.

'This will give you lots of energy for all that fun you're going to have,' smiled Kanga.

'Yummy!' Roo exclaimed happily.

As soon as he had finished, Roo dashed outside to meet his friends.

Everyone had finished work by the time Roo found them. Eeyore's house was as good as new again.

'Now we can play!' shouted Roo. Rabbit had an idea. 'Let's have a sack race!'

Everyone scrambled about, climbing into big canvas sacks. Piglet and Roo shared one, and Pooh and Tigger were in another, with Eeyore following behind on his own.

'Let's race!' cried Roo.

'Ready… Set… GO!' Owl yelled, and everyone jumped forward as fast as they could go.

20

'We're winning! We're winning!' cried Roo, as he and Piglet jumped over the finishing line.

'My stomach feels all bouncy,' whined Piglet. 'It hurts!' He clutched his wobbly tummy.

'Bouncing's difficult when you've got a sack around you,' protested Tigger, out of breath. 'It's makin' me so very tired.'

'That was fun!' giggled Roo, 'Come on, let's do it again!'

But everyone except Roo had collapsed into a pile on the ground. They were much too tired to start another race.

Roo smiled. 'Sleeping in the day isn't so silly after all,' he said. 'Next time we should all take a nap!'

But his friends were sound asleep already…